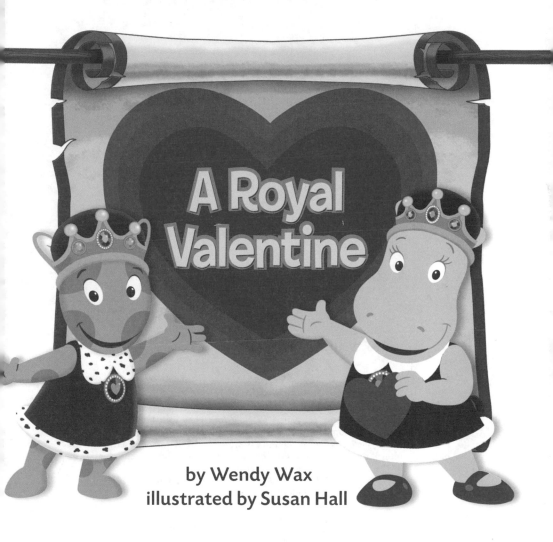

A Royal Valentine

by Wendy Wax
illustrated by Susan Hall

Ready-to-Read

SIMON SPOTLIGHT/NICKELODEON
New York   London   Toronto   Sydney

Based on the TV series *Nick Jr. The Backyardigans*™ as seen on Nick Jr.®

SIMON SPOTLIGHT
An imprint of Simon & Schuster Children's Publishing Division
1230 Avenue of the Americas, New York, New York 10020
© 2006 Viacom International Inc. All rights reserved. NICK JR.,
Nick Jr. The Backyardigans, and all related titles, logos, and characters are trademarks
of Viacom International Inc. All rights reserved, including the right of reproduction in
whole or in part in any form.
SIMON SPOTLIGHT, READY-TO-READ, and colophon
are registered trademarks of Simon & Schuster, Inc.
Manufactured in the United States of America
4 6 8 10 9 7 5
Library of Congress Cataloging-in-Publication Data
Wax, Wendy.
A Royal Valentine / by Wendy Wax; illustrated by Susan Hall.—1st ed.
p. cm.—(Ready-to-read)
"Based on the TV series Nick Jr. The Backyardigans as seen on Nick Jr."
ISBN-13: 978-1-4169-0801-2 (pbk.)
ISBN-10: 1-4169-0801-3 (pbk.)
I. Hall, Susan, 1940- II. Title. III. Series.
PZ7.W35117Roy 2006
[E]—dc22
2005012110

Meet Queen !
TASHA

Queen  made a
TASHA   VALENTINE

for her best friend,

Queen .
UNIQUA

 and will bring

TYRONE   PABLO

the to Queen

VALENTINE   UNIQUA

in her far away.

PALACE

"Nothing can stop us!"

says .

TYRONE

"Not  , or 🌨,
WIND   SNOW
or the 〰 wide!"
        RIVER
🐧 says.
PABLO

The blows.

WIND

"This is strong,"

WIND

says .

PABLO

" will not stop us!"
WIND

says .

TYRONE

 starts to fall.

SNOW

" will not stop us!"

SNOW

says .

PABLO

"I have .
GOGGLES

Now we can see the ."
PATH

"There is a wide ," says .

RIVER

PABLO

"How will we cross?"

"I know!"  says.

TYRONE

"We will jump across on

the blocks of ⬜."

ICE

"Nothing can stop us!" say  and .

PABLO TYRONE

"Not , or , or the

WIND SNOW

wide!"

RIVER

"Queen 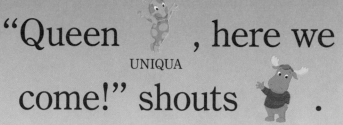, here we come!" shouts .

UNIQUA

TYRONE

At last and

TYRONE   PABLO

reach the .

PALACE

They knock on the .

DOOR

"Who is there?" asks ,

AUSTIN

the guard.

PALACE

"Queen sent us,"
TASHA

say and .
PABLO   TYRONE

"Come in," says .
AUSTIN

"Special  delivery for
VALENTINE

Queen  from Queen ,"
UNIQUA   TASHA

call  and  .
PABLO   TYRONE

"Wow!" says Queen .
UNIQUA

"I love it!

I have something

for Queen , too."
TASHA

"We will bring it to her,"
 says.

"Nothing can stop us!"

says .

"I must give it to

Queen myself,"

TASHA

says Queen .

UNIQUA

"I want to go too!" says.

AUSTIN

Queen ,
 , and
UNIQUA
AUSTIN   PABLO   TYRONE
go to see Queen .
TASHA

"Special delivery for

Queen ,"
TASHA

says Queen .
UNIQUA

"What is it?" asks

Queen .
TASHA

"It is a big hug.

Happy Valentine's Day!"